COMES A WIND

by **Linda Arms White**   pictures by **Tom Curry**

Dorling Kindersley Publishing, Inc.

For my sister, Sharon Arms Doucet, who plays
Clement to my Clyde, and our mother, Miriam,
who still hopes one day we'll get along—L. W.

For Mom—T. C.

DK
Ink

A Melanie Kroupa Book
Dorling Kindersley Publishing, Inc.
95 Madison Avenue
New York, New York 10016

Visit us on the World Wide Web at http://www.dk.com

Dorling Kindersley books are available at special discounts for bulk purchases for
sales promotions or premiums. Special editions, including personalized covers,
excerpts of existing guides, and corporate imprints can be created in large quantities
for specific needs. For more information, contact
Special Markets Dept., Dorling Kindersley Publishing, Inc.,
95 Madison Ave., New York, NY 10016; fax: (800) 600-9098.

Library of Congress Cataloging-in-Publication Data

White, Linda Arms.
    Comes a wind / by Linda Arms White ; pictures by Tom Curry. —1st ed.
        p.   cm.
    Summary: While visiting their mother's ranch, two brothers who
constantly try to best each other swap tall tales about big winds and are
surprised by the fiercest wind they have ever seen.
    ISBN 0-7894-2601-3
    [1. Winds—Fiction. 2. Brothers—Fiction. 3. Tall tales.]
    I. Curry, Tom, ill. II. Title.
    PZ7.W58387Co   2000
    [E]—dc21   98-47170
                                                CIP
                                                AC

Book design by Chris Hammill Paul. The illustrations for this book were painted
with acrylics. The text of this book is set in 20 point Gloucester Old Style.

Printed and bound in U.S.A.

First Edition, 2000
10 9 8 7 6 5 4 3 2

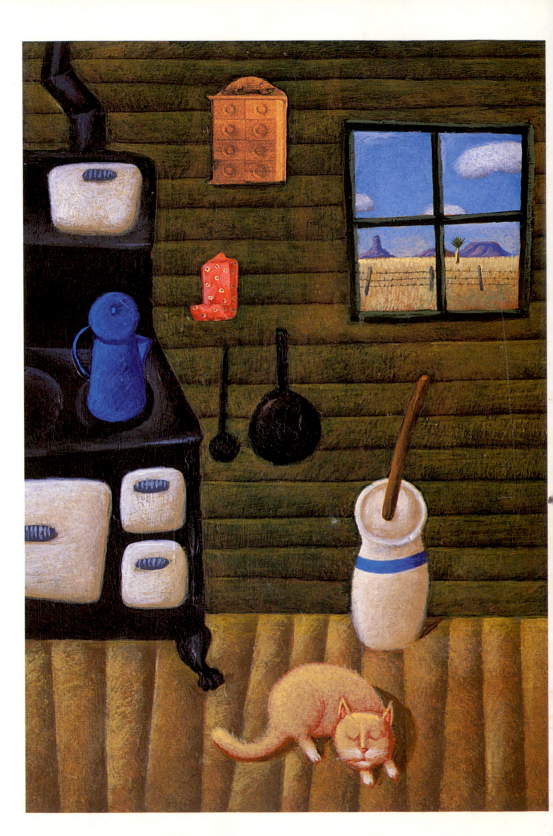

Mama licked her pencil and started writing:

Dear Clement and Clyde,
You boys are so peas-in-a-pod alike, it's beyond me why you always have to outshine each other. My birthday's round the corner, and I'm pining for only one thing. Just once, I'd like to pass the day with you two boys and no squabblin'!

Honor your mama's wishes and come home to the ranch Monday week. No presents. Just you and your brother being nice to each other.

Love,
Your mama

Ever since they were little, Clement and Clyde had tried to best each other.

When Clement learned to roast a hot dog nice and even over a camp fire, Clyde served up a five-course meal complete with apple pie cooked on a stick.

When Clyde figured out how to rope a bucking bronco, Clement managed to ride one—bareback.

And when Clement decided to raise the biggest pig at the county fair in order to win a blue ribbon, Clyde raised a bigger one and taught it to dance a jig and join in the "E-I-E-I-O" as he sang "Old MacDonald Had a Farm."

Mama had hoped it would stop when Clement and Clyde became grown-ups, but things only got worse.

On Mama's birthday, Clement drove up in his racehorse-sleek, midnight black pickup truck with the patent leather interior. He climbed out and, slapping his ten-gallon hat atop his head, shambled toward the house like a hound dog on its way to a flea dip.

Clement's dust hadn't settled before Clyde roared up in his longhorned, rooster red pickup truck with the genuine steer hide interior. He clambered out and, putting a fifteen-gallon hat atop his head, shuffled toward the house like a calf on the end of a branding rope.

"Happy birthday, Mama," each mumbled, glaring at the other.

"Thanks for comin', boys," Mama said, hands on her hips. "Come set a spell on the porch. I'll fetch us some nice cold lemonade. With extra sugar," she added, looking at them.

Clement and Clyde propped their spit-shined, high-heeled, pointy-toed boots up on the rail. Neither could think of a single Mama-pleasing thing to say.

But just then a breeze came up and gave the windmill a gentle turn.

Squeak, squeak, squeak.

"Looks like it comes a wind," said Clement.

"You call that a wind?" grumbled Clyde. "Why, one day it was so windy, it ripped our clothes plumb off the line, scattering them clear across Lariat County. My Mimi's dainties landed on that Texas Ranger statue in front of town hall. Now *that* was a wind!"

Now, Clement didn't want to spoil Mama's birthday, but when he caught sight of the smirk on his brother's face, there was no way he could keep from adding his two cents.

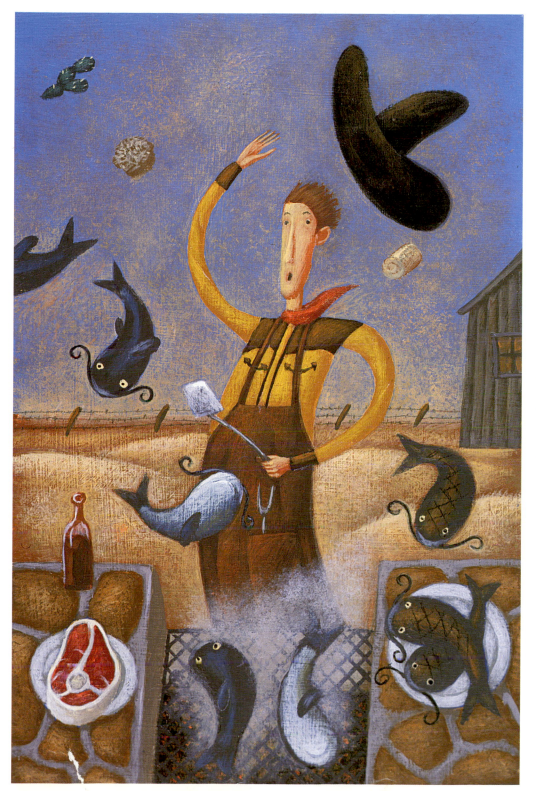

"That's not a wind!" snapped Clement. "Why, one day it was so windy, it churned a mess of trout right out of the crick. Plopped them on the grate I had ready for barbecuin', then blew the other way five minutes later and flipped them over. Cooked to perfection, they was. Now *that* was a wind!"

Clyde opened his mouth, but just then Mama called from the kitchen, "I know it's hard for you boys to get along. I appreciate your trying a heap."

"Yes, Mama," they muttered.

Clyde clamped his jaw tight and swallowed hard. But the words shot out of him like a cork out of hot sody water.

"That's not a wind. One day it was so windy, it stretched the telephone lines down my road all the way to Rattlesnake Hill. Next day when I called my neighbor, the phone company charged me for a long-distance call. Now *that* was a wind!"

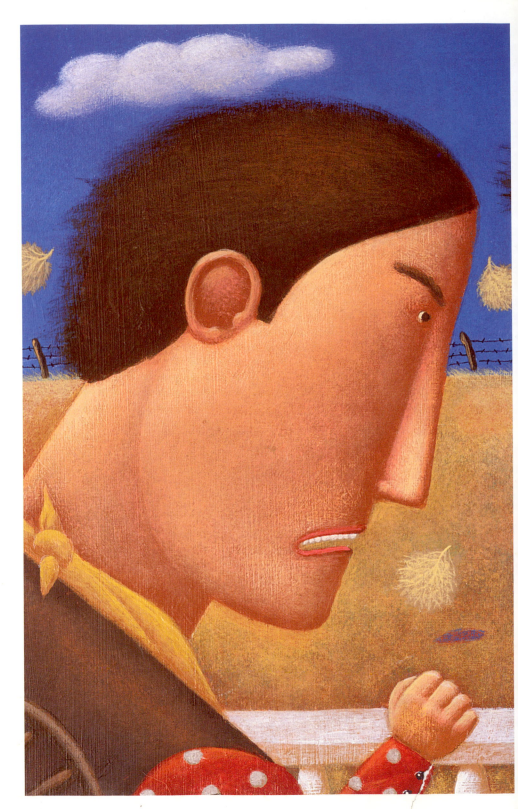

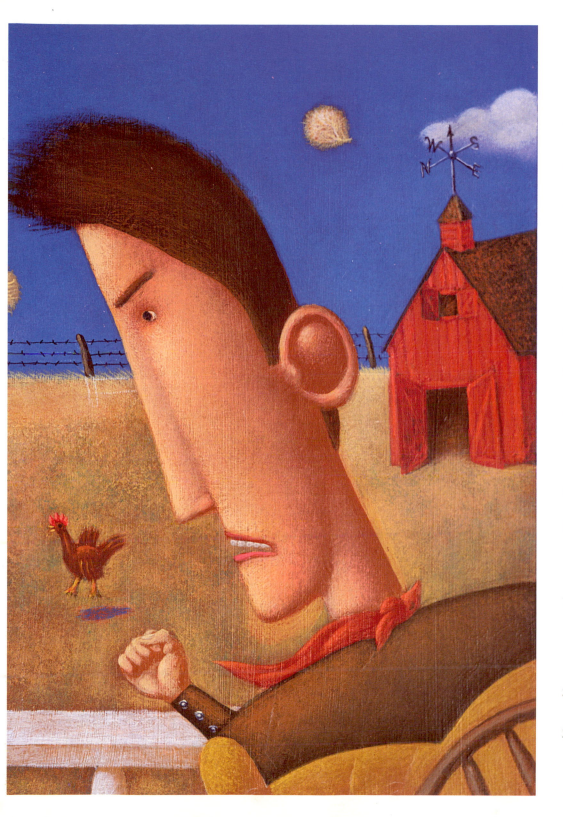

"Yeah? Well, one day it was so windy," Clement barked, "it whipped round Muleskin Knob and couldn't get straightened out. Got to doin' loop-de-loops over the poultry yard. My prize goose laid the same egg three times. When I cracked it open, that egg was already scrambled. *That* was a wind!"

"You call that a wind?" Clyde asked. But before he could say more, Clement stopped him.

"Now, listen here, it's Mama's birthday. We gotta stop this."

"All right. For Mama. Just nobody say no more about the wind," Clyde grunted.

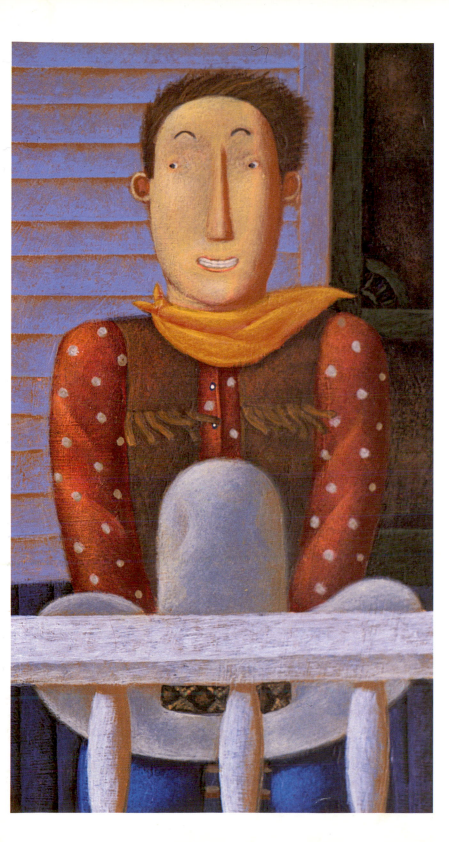

Mama came out and set the lemonade
pitcher and glasses on the porch rail.
"Havin' you boys get along makes me
happy as an armadillo with an anthill all
her own. I baked a little cake to celebrate.
I'll get it." She patted their heads and
opened the door.

Squeak, squeak, squeak

went the windmill.

"Looks like it comes a wind,"
Mama said as she disappeared back into
the house.

"That does it. One day it was so windy," Clyde snapped, "it plucked every last feather off my chickens. Shamed 'em so, Mimi had to knit 'em little woollies to wear till their feathers grew back. Now *that* was a wind!"

"That's not a wind!" boomed Clement. "One day it was so windy, it whooshed through the high school marching band, caught the bell of my boy's tuba, and screwed him twelve feet into the ground. Took the whole football team and the water boy to pull him back out. Now *that* was a wind!"

"You call that a wind?" Clyde began. "One day it was so—"

Just then the sky turned dusty red.

The wind snatched Clyde's words out of his mouth.

It yanked the buttons from Clement's shirt.

It blew the leaves right off the trees.

Clement and Clyde had to grab hold of the porch rail to keep from blowing straight to Kansas. Their eyes grew bigger than hen's eggs when they saw twenty-three acres of tumbleweed and a flock of chickens whirl by—beaks, wings, feathers, and all.

Right on their tails was a two-hole outhouse, doors flapping like the wings of a dizzy duck.

The wind mounted. Clement and Clyde held tight as their feet were pried up from the floorboards. Their eyes grew bigger than goose eggs when they saw a whole herd of longhorns—cows, steers, and a huge, speckled bull—blacken the sky. Those longhorns tumbled end over end. Their mouths hung open, bawling, but their bellows had long since blown by.

The wind whipped around. Clement and Clyde clung fast to the rail, stretched head-to-toe like arrows on a weather vane. Their eyes grew bigger than ostrich eggs when they saw Clement's red barn whip past, horses still in their stalls, kittens still in the loft. Right behind scuttled twenty miles of barbed-wire fence and Clyde's hay baler, baling mile after mile of prickly pears, sagebrush, and mesquite trees.

Mama came to the door with the cake.

"No, Mama, don't —" the boys shouted.

But it was too late. When she stepped out on the porch, the wind caught her skirt. It billowed out like a ship's sail at full mast. Away she shot over Clement's racehorse-sleek pickup and Clyde's longhorned one, around the scarecrow, past the garden shed, and over the barn.

Suddenly the wind stopped.

Mama plummeted out of the sky. Next thing she knew her skirt had caught on the rickety weather vane atop the barn. "Help, boys. Git me down!" she cried, flapping like a broody hen.

Clement and Clyde sprang into action. Clement wrestled the ladder from the barn.

Clyde climbed to the top and boosted Clement to the roof.

Clement pulled Clyde up.

Together, they scrambled to the peak and, without even stopping to bicker over who should go first, shinnied up the weather vane.

Mama grinned ear to ear, watching her boys working like two mules hitched to the same load.

Then Clyde cut Mama loose and
Clement caught her, gentle as you please.
The three of them collapsed onto
the roof.

"Now *that* —" said Clement.

"—was a wind!" said Clyde.